This Little Tiger book belongs to:

_____

_____

_____

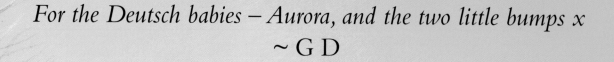

For the Deutsch babies – Aurora, and the two little bumps x
~ G D

For my lovely friend, Dianne
~ A E

LITTLE TIGER PRESS LTD,
an imprint of the Little Tiger Group
1 Coda Studios, 189 Munster Road, London SW6 6AW
www.littletiger.co.uk

First published in Great Britain 2018
This edition published 2019

Text by Georgiana Deutsch
Text copyright © Little Tiger Press Ltd 2018
Illustrations copyright © Alison Edgson 2018
Alison Edgson has asserted her right to be identified
as the author and illustrator of this work under the
Copyright, Designs and Patents Act, 1988
A CIP catalogue record for this book is available from the British Library

ISBN 978-1-84869-948-9
Printed in China
LTP/1800/2654/0519
10 9 8 7 6 5 4 3 2 1

The Snow Rabbit

Georgiana Deutsch   Alison Edgson

LiTTLE TiGER

LONDON

Bear was ALWAYS GRUMPY.
He had a big, furry frown and a sulky scowl.
And whenever he felt EXTRA SPECIALLY
grumpy, he would give a grizzly, grumbly . . .

GR

RRRRROWL!
Shhhhh!
Bear's in a REALLY bad mood!
ONLY BEARS ALLOWED

The animals didn't dare to go near Bear's beautiful garden. Except for one very smiley Rabbit . . .

"Poor Bear," thought Rabbit, as she skipped away. "He needs cheering up!" And Rabbit knew just what to do!

Don't do it, Rabbit!

I've got a brilliant idea!

That night, Bear couldn't sleep.
He grouched and grumbled and
looked out of his window. And there,
in the moonlight, was . . .

The trees trembled and shook at the sound of Bear's rumbling roar, until . . . CRASH!

A dollop of snow landed right on top of Bear *and* the snow rabbit!

The next morning, Bear woke up in a
VERY BAD MOOD. He peeked
outside, frowning as he saw the wonky
snow rabbit sitting sadly in the sunshine.

I told Rabbit
this was a bad idea!

"FOX!" Bear growled. "Did YOU build a snow rabbit in MY garden?" Fox gulped. "N-n-n-no!" he stuttered. Bear harrumphed and stomped off. "It must have been Badger," he grumbled.

Bear stormed up Badger's garden path.

"RIGHT!" roared Bear.
"If it wasn't Fox or Badger,
and it wasn't the squirrels,
it must have been . . ."

...RABBIT!

"Hello, Bear!" smiled Rabbit, hopping up. "Did you call?"
"YES!" bellowed Bear. "YOU put a snow rabbit in my garden!"

I can't watch!

"I-I-I thought it might make you smile!" said Rabbit, hopefully.
Bear took a deep breath.
The animals covered their ears.
"Well, it did NOT make me smile,"
Bear growled . . .

Poor Rabbit!

Eeek!

"IT MADE A MASSIVE MESS! And you're going to help me fix it! OR ELSE!" Bear turned and marched home. Rabbit blinked in amazement.

"We can mend this!" Rabbit beamed when
she saw the squashed snow rabbit.
And, together, that's what they did.

Then, when the snow rabbit looked perfectly perfect,
they made a snow bear. And for the first time
in a long time, Bear forgot to be grumpy.

That night, Bear couldn't sleep. He stood at his window and gazed down at the snow bear and the snow rabbit, standing together in the moonlight. A slow smile spread across Bear's face. "It feels good to have a friend," he thought.

And that gave Bear a WONDERFUL IDEA.

Chuckling to himself,
Bear pulled on his
boots . . .

marched into his perfect
garden . . .

I'd better
change THIS!

and set to work on
his mysterious plan.

The next morning, the animals were in for a surprise . . .

And with so many new friends,
Bear was NEVER grumpy again!